The Colors of the Chameleon

Please visit our web site at: www.garethstevens.com
For a free color catalog describing Gareth Stevens Publishing's
list of high-quality books and multimedia programs, call
1-800-542-2595 or fax your request to (414) 332-3567.

Library of Congress Cataloging-in-Publication Data

Benevelli, Alberto.
    [Colore del camaleonte. English]
    The colors of the chameleon / written by Alberto Benevelli;
illustrated by Loretta Serofilli.
        p. cm.
    Summary: Of all the animals who live in the shade of the palm trees,
the chameleon is very special because he can change his color at any time.
    ISBN 0-8368-3042-3 (lib. bdg.)
    [1. Chameleons—Fiction.   2. Animals—Fiction.   3. Color—Fiction.]
I. Serofilli, Loretta, ill.   II. Title.
PZ7.B43327Co   2002
[E]—dc21   2001054219

This North American edition first published in 2002 by
Gareth Stevens Publishing
A World Almanac Education Group Company
330 West Olive Street, Suite 100
Milwaukee, Wisconsin 53212 USA

This U.S. edition © 2002 by Gareth Stevens, Inc.
First published as *Il colore del camaleonte* © 1997 Edizioni Arka-Milano/Italy.

Gareth Stevens editor: Dorothy L. Gibbs

Printed in the United States of America

1 2 3 4 5 6 7 8 9 06 05 04 03 02

The Colors of the Chameleon

by Alberto Benevelli
Illustrated by Loretta Serofilli

Gareth Stevens Publishing
A WORLD ALMANAC EDUCATION GROUP COMPANY

The African desert is very, very hot. The riverbank is the only place where trees grow and animals can go to cool off and have a drink of water.

A monkey, a zebra, a giraffe, and a chameleon lived on the riverbank in the shade of the palm trees. The monkey was all gray. The zebra had black and white stripes. The giraffe was yellow with brown spots. The chameleon . . . well, the chameleon was very, very special. He changed color all the time!

The monkey, the zebra, and the giraffe loved to look at the chameleon. Every time the chameleon changed color, they "oohed" and "aahed" in wonder.

One day, the monkey asked the chameleon, "Which color is the best?"

"Yes," said the zebra and the giraffe, "you are the color expert. Tell us which color is the nicest."

The chameleon thought and thought, but he could not come up with an answer. "All of the colors are nice," he thought, "how can I choose which one is the best?"

From the riverbank, the chameleon could see the brightly colored fish swimming in the water.

"Tell me," he asked the fish, "which color is the nicest?"

But fish have no voices. They could not give the chameleon an answer.

10

11

By nightfall, the chameleon still had not decided, so the monkey said, "Look at my fur. Do you think gray is the nicest color?"

"Gray!" said the zebra. "Gray is dull and ordinary. Look at my beautiful black and white stripes."

"Your stripes are not as beautiful and colorful as my yellow with brown spots," said the giraffe.

The chameleon looked at each of the animals carefully, but their colors all seemed equally beautiful.

Soon, the monkey, the zebra, and the giraffe started quarreling.

"There's no doubt about it," said the monkey angrily, "my color is the most beautiful."

"No, it isn't!" screamed the zebra. "Mine is."

"No!" shouted the giraffe. "Mine is!"

14

The animals quarreled all night long.

At dawn, a crocodile, who was not able to sleep a wink all night with all the screaming and shouting, thought to himself, "What a silly quarrel! Now that I can see all these animals better, I am certain that my color is the nicest."

The crocodile swam up close to the riverbank and shouted, "Go away! You are all so ugly I never want to see you again. From now on, I will share the river only with animals who are green like me!"

Then the crocodile opened his enormous jaws and flashed his razor-sharp teeth. The monkey, the zebra, and the giraffe were so frightened they ran away. They left the shade of the palm trees and hid behind the sand dunes in the desert.

The chameleon stayed on the riverbank. The crocodile did not notice him because the chameleon had changed into the color of the stones and the sand.

Before too long, the chameleon started to miss his friends. One day, he had an idea. He jumped onto the crocodile's back, and his color turned green.

"Look, crocodile," he said, "I am green, just like you. Can I stay here on the riverbank?"

"Yes," said the crocodile. "You are green, so you can stay here with me. I'm very glad you are here to keep me company. I was starting to get bored all by myself."

"I know lots of other animals like me," said the chameleon. "We should invite them to stay here, too. The riverbank will be much nicer with even more animals."

"What a wonderful idea!" exclaimed the crocodile. "If the other animals are like you, I will gladly share the riverbank with them, too."

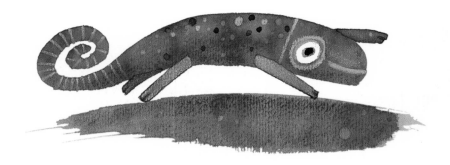

Without delay, the chameleon ran toward the desert.

He found the monkey, the zebra, and the giraffe hiding behind the sand dunes. The Sun was scorching, and the animals were thirsty and exhausted from the heat.

"Follow me," the chameleon said to them.

When the animals got to the riverbank, the chameleon jumped onto the monkey's back and turned gray. "Look, crocodile," he said. "The monkey is just like me."

Then the chameleon jumped onto the zebra and turned black and white — in stripes! "Look, crocodile," he said. "The zebra is just like me."

Finally, he jumped onto the giraffe and turned yellow with brown spots. "The giraffe is like me, too. So we can all stay on the riverbank with you."

The crocodile became very angry when he saw all the animals he had sent away. But then, he remembered the promise he had made. So the monkey, the zebra, and the giraffe returned to the riverbank, shouting and splashing with joy.

Still, the crocodile was upset. He did not like to look at animals that were so different from him.

"The chameleon tricked me," said the crocodile, grinding his teeth. "He is not green anymore."

"That's not true," said the chameleon, sliding onto a leaf. "Anyway, what does it matter? Before the animals came back, the riverbank was a sad and lonely place. Now it is full of life and many beautiful colors."

The crocodile looked around and noticed that the riverbank really had changed. He saw the animals playing and having fun in the water. The crocodile got into the water, too, and with a thrash of his enormous tail, he made a huge wave. The monkey applauded. The zebra cheered. The giraffe shouted, "More! More!" So the crocodile made another wave for them.

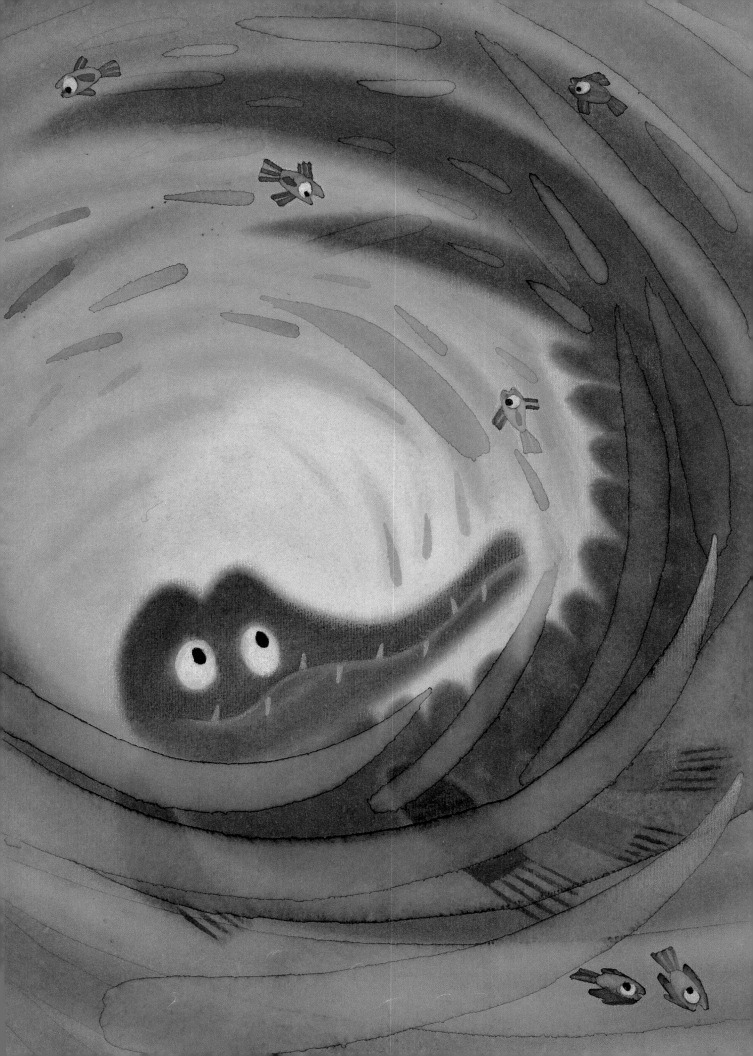

Since that day, there have been lots of waves and
splashes in the river. The crocodile makes some of them.
The monkey, the zebra, and the giraffe make some, too.
The droplets of water that spray into the air sparkle with
the colors of all the animals. The colors form a gigantic
rainbow in the sky.

Admiring the rainbow, the chameleon was finally able to decide which color was the nicest.

"About time!" said the monkey.

"Which color is it?" asked the zebra, the giraffe, and the crocodile.

"Mine!" answered the chameleon. "Because my color is a combination of all of your colors."

"That's true," the animals agreed. "Yours is the best color of all!"